The Invisible String

Patrice Karst ♥ Illustrated by Joanne Lew-Vriethoff

LB

Little, Brown and Company

New York   Boston

Little, Brown and Company
Hachette Book Group
1290 Avenue of the Americas, New York, NY 10104
Visit us at LBYR.com

Text originally published in 2000 by DeVorss & Company, Publishers, in the United States of America
First Paperback Edition: October 2018

Little, Brown and Company is a division of Hachette Book Group, Inc. The Little, Brown name and logo are trademarks of Hachette Book Group, Inc.

The publisher is not responsible for websites (or their content) that are not owned by the publisher.

Library of Congress Catalog Card Number 00-130314
ISBN: 978-0-316-48623-1 (pbk.)

Printed in China

1010

10 9 8 7 6 5 4 3 2 1

The illustrations for this book were created digitally. This book was designed by Jen Keenan.
The production was supervised by Erika Schwartz, and the production editor was Annie McDonnell.
The text was set in Shannon, and the display type is Gulyesa.

To the children of the world,
and the magic of their Strings . . .

Liza and Jeremy, the twins, were asleep one calm and quiet night.

Suddenly it began to rain very hard. Thunder rumbled until it got so loud that it woke them up.

"Mommy, Mommy!" they cried out as they ran to her.

"Don't worry, you two! It's just the storm making all that noise. Go back to bed."

"We want to stay close to you," said Jeremy. "We're scared!"

Mom said, *"You know we're always together, no matter what."*

"But how can we be together when you're out here and we're in bed?" said Liza.

Mom held something right in front of them and said,

"This is how."

Rubbing their sleepy eyes, the twins came closer to see what Mom was holding.

"I was about your age when my mommy first told me about

the INVISIBLE STRING."

"I don't see a string," said Jeremy.

"You don't need to see the Invisible String. People who love each other are always connected by

a very special String made of love."

"But if you can't see it, how do you know it's there?" asked Liza.

"Even though you can't see it with your eyes, you can feel it with your heart and know that you are

always connected to everyone you love."

"When you're at school and you miss me, your love travels all the way along the String until I feel it tug on my heart."

"And when you tug it right back, we feel it in our hearts," said Jeremy.

"Does Jasper the cat have an Invisible String?" Liza asked.

"She sure does," said Mom.

"And best friends like me and Lucy?" asked Liza.

"Best friends too!"

"How far can the String reach?"

"Would it reach me even if I were a submarine captain deep in the ocean?" asked Jeremy.

"Yes," Mom said. "Even there."

"A dancer in France?"

"Even there."

"A jungle explorer?"

"Even there."

"How about an astronaut out in space?"

"Yes, even there."

Then Jeremy quietly asked, "Can my String reach all the way to Uncle Brian in heaven?"

"Yes, even there."

"Does the String go away when you're mad at us?"

"Never," said Mom. "Love is stronger than anger, and as long as love is in your heart,

the String will always be there."

"Even when you get older and can't agree
about things like what movie to see . . .

. . . or what game to play in the back seat . . .

. . . or what time to go to bed.

Oh, that's right! You two should be in bed!"

And with that, they all laughed as Mom
chased the twins back to their beds.

Within a few minutes, they were asleep, even though the storm was still making the same loud noises outside.

As they slept, they started dreaming of all **the Invisible Strings** they have,

and all the Strings their friends have,

and their friends have,

and their friends have,

and their friends have,

. . . no one is ever alone.

A WORD FROM THE AUTHOR

Dear Beloved Reader,

I am honored to tell you the backstory of how this little-book-that-could came to life. *The Invisible String* was born in 1996, when I was a full-time working single mom. As I dropped off my son, Elijah, at preschool each morning, he would cry so hard that it broke my heart. And so I told him what was obvious to me: that an Invisible String made out of love always connected us. In fact, not only would it connect us all day long, but forever and ever—no matter what!

Voilà! Once he knew about the String, his separation anxiety stopped, his face lit up in wonder, and his tears dried. The story brought him (and then his friends, who begged to hear it, too) immense comfort with the realization that they would never be alone, because the Invisible String connects us not only to our loved ones but also to the whole wide world.

When I saw the reaction that the Invisible String was having on these children, I knew I needed to "tell the others." I went to a small independent publisher to see if he was interested, and he released the original hardcover edition in 2000. Slowly, I began to receive the most powerful and profound letters from readers about how *The Invisible String* had affected them and the people with whom they had shared the book. My heart could not have felt more full.

Several years ago, though, I noticed a new phenomenon beginning. *The Invisible String* suddenly started to move, then sprint—and the next thing I knew, it took off and soared, becoming a bestseller. In addition to receiving countless testimonials from the general public, I continue to hear weekly from schools, bereavement groups, psychologists, military personnel, hospitals, camp counselors, therapists, hospices, funeral homes, adoption and foster organizations, divorce attorney's offices, prisons, and parenting classes about how *The Invisible String* is being used to guide, comfort, and heal. Beyond assisting children and adults with any type of loss or separation issues, readers tell me they appreciate how it offers a tangible understanding of what the abstract concept of love is. For the science-loving fans, I like to say it's "String theory made easy!" Even adults are giving the book to each other for birthdays, shower gifts, and going-away presents for family, friends, and spouses—any time they want to share the love! No one is too young or too old to know of their Invisible Strings.

While there is only a single word on one page in the book that alludes to separation by death, it has been astonishing to witness how it has opened up the possibilities for the story to be used for coping with grief. That word, *heaven*, is not meant to impart any particular religious affiliation in mind, heart, or meaning, for my readers come from all faiths, spiritual paths, and walks of life. It is a word that for so many readers open-endedly suggests "the other side" or "the great beyond" or the indefinable mystery of permanent physical departure. For those that feel uncomfortable with that word, it is easily amended with whatever phrase feels more comfortable for each family, and can be used as a springboard for further discussion. And remember that there is nothing more healing than conversation with a child, if questions arise.

We live in tumultuous times, to say the least. But what affects one of us, affects the whole of us. One of my greatest hopes is to see world leaders coming to the realization that we are ultimately one family. I know that can happen because love really is that powerful, and the Invisible String is the realest thing that there is. It transcends time and space, reaching across the planet and beyond. Where all of our Invisible Strings intersect, we find ourselves in the *real* "worldwide Web" that collectively forms the nest that holds us close. The more love, the more Invisible Strings, and the more Strings, the stronger our Invisible Web.

My vision is that one day, every child on earth will be comforted by knowing of their own Invisible Strings. One heart at a time, I believe that day will come sooner than we realize. To that end, if you feel moved by your Invisible Strings, please "tell the others"!

With all my heart and all that I am, and wherever in the world this book has found you, I send love from my end of the Invisible String, over to you . . .

Patrice Karst

ACKNOWLEDGMENTS

To everyone along the way who has helped spread the message of the Invisible String, too many to name—you are ALL a part of this phenomenon of love soaring around the world, one heart at a time.

To those that I love and are traveling the planet alongside me, you make everything worth it. And our Strings will connect us for all time, so there!

To Michelle Zeitlin and Jane Cowen Hamilton at More Zap Literary, my agents extraordinaire—you were the answer to my many years of prayers. Thank you to the moon and beyond for showing up.

To Andrea Spooner and everyone at Little, Brown Books for Young Readers, thank you for allowing the love of the Invisible String to weave its magic around you and for reintroducing these wondrous Strings onto the world stage.

To my dazzling illustrator, Joanne Lew-Vriethoff, for your gift of art that brings the message of my words into a spellbinding visual landscape. I cried the first time I saw your work.

To the other end of my most important String, my son, Elijah, thank you for all that you are and for teaching me all that I am. This book was born because your momma loves you so much that it could be explained in no other way.

To the little girl inside me for believing in love no matter what and for being so, so brave.

To Coco the Magical Weiner Dog for being the best antidepressant on four legs.

To every single one of the amazing groups, clubs, camps, and organizations that have helped spread the word about the Invisible String and to every parent, caregiver, teacher, therapist, and childcare worker, thank you for never forgetting that love comes first and everything else second . . . Because of you, the world is finding out about their very own Invisible Strings.

To the leaders across the globe, please read this book and act accordingly. Perhaps it takes a children's book to help you see that we are all connected. We are ONE, and it is time to heal our planet.

To God for it ALL . . . To Love and Her Strings . . . To You . . .

Patrice Karst